The Power of Kindness

Through the Eyes of Children

By **Ruth Maille**
Art by **Pencil Master Studio**

Illustrations by Pardeep Mehra
Designed by Priyam Mehra

Publisher's Cataloging-in-Publication data

Names: Maille, Ruth, author. | Mehra, Pardeep, illustrator.
Title: The power of kindness / by Ruth Maille ; illustrated by Pardeep Mehra.
Series: The Power Of
Description: Bristol, RI: Orbit Publishing, 2021. | Orbit visits a kindergarten classroom to look for examples of kindness in everyday life.
Identifiers: LCCN: 2021906155 | ISBN 978-1-955299-01-5 (hardcover) | 978-1-955299-02-2 (paperback) | 978-1-955299-00-8 (ebook)
Subjects: LCSH Kindergarten--Juvenile fiction. | School--Juvenile fiction. | Kindness--Juvenile fiction. | CYAC Kindergarten--Fiction. | School--Fiction. | Kindness--Fiction. | BISAC JUVENILE FICTION / Social Themes / Values & Virtues | JUVENILE FICTION / General
Classification: LCC PZ7.1.M346825 Po 2021 | DDC [E]--dc23

Dedication

This journey has been so amazing. If it were not for some very special people, none of this could be possible.

I am grateful for my fantastic editor, **Bobbie Hinman**, who tweaked just the right words to make my story flow. To **April Cox** and her program, **Self Publishing made Simple**, who has shared her knowledge and expertise every step of the way. My illustrator **Pardeep Mehra**, with his creativity and ability to think outside the box and willingness to try something new, made my story come to life. **Priyam Mehra** and the **Pencil Master** team worked magic with color design and placement of words. It has been a pleasure partnering with these unique and outstanding individuals.

A special thanks to **Diane Lawbaugh**, an incredible friend who helped me brainstorm and edit my rough drafts. Her love and support are the epitome of kindness.

To my BFF's **Cathy Hudson** and **Paula Hanson**, for their ability to hold the basket as I spill my self-doubt and then see the true picture of how my books are helping children worldwide.

Kindness is the Way!

Hi kids, listen up!
Today we need to talk about
Kindness!
How about you tell me what that is?

Sure!

Kindness is a thing you do
When you have a friend who's feeling blue
You ask them about their day
You hug them to make them feel okay!

That's right!
Kindness is the way!
Yaaaay!

Ok now, listen up
Who can tell me more about
Kindness and other ways
We can be nice today?

Kindness is when you see a dog
Being all alone, hungry and cold
You take him to your home
and make sure that he's warm

And you let him stay because
Kindness is the way! Yaaaay!

Hey Orbit!
Would you like to share this chocolate bar
with me?
Oh, thank you, you're so kind!
The pleasure is all mine!

Cause kindness is when we share
When we show how much we care!
No matter how great or small
An act of kindness is always good!

Kindness is giving back to others
Open the doors or help carry a load
Kindness is choosing to be selfless
So let's help the ones who need it the most!

So spread kindness! La la la la!
Spread kindness every day!
Spread kindness! La la la la!
Let me hear you say
Kindness is the way! Yaaay!

Visit https://www.ruthmaille-author.com/the-power-of-kindness and follow the song as you sing along.
Look for more The Power of ... books with Orbit at www.ruthmaille-author.com
The Power of Positivity The ABCs of a Pandemic
The Power of Gratitude There is Always Something to be Grateful For

Hello friends,

Are you wondering why Orbit has two band-aids on his head?

You see, Orbit was born during the pandemic when our world was hurting. Just like when you get hurt, sometimes putting a band-aid on your boo-boo helps to make you feel better. Orbit's band-aids remind us that his adventures are about helping our world heal by teaching children ways to make life better for themselves and the people around them. He wants every child to know how they can play a big part in healing our world by spreading positivity, kindness, and love. Orbit knows he can't heal our world by himself. He needs every child to join him on his adventures so that together we can make the world a more loving and kind place in which to live.

Love

Ruth

Introduction

This book was inspired by a group of children in my daycare & preschool. While having a snack one day, I asked them where they felt kindness in their lives. Their examples are as unique as the children themselves. As you read this book, I hope you will love looking at kindness through their eyes.

As the sun rises high in the sky, Orbit is busy planning his day. He is on a mission to spread kindness to everyone.

His first stop is a kindergarten class. When he arrives, the children are excited to see him. As they sit on the brightly-colored rug, Orbit asks the children, "What is kindness?"

WHAT IS
Kindness?

Hands fly in the air. The children shout out their ideas.

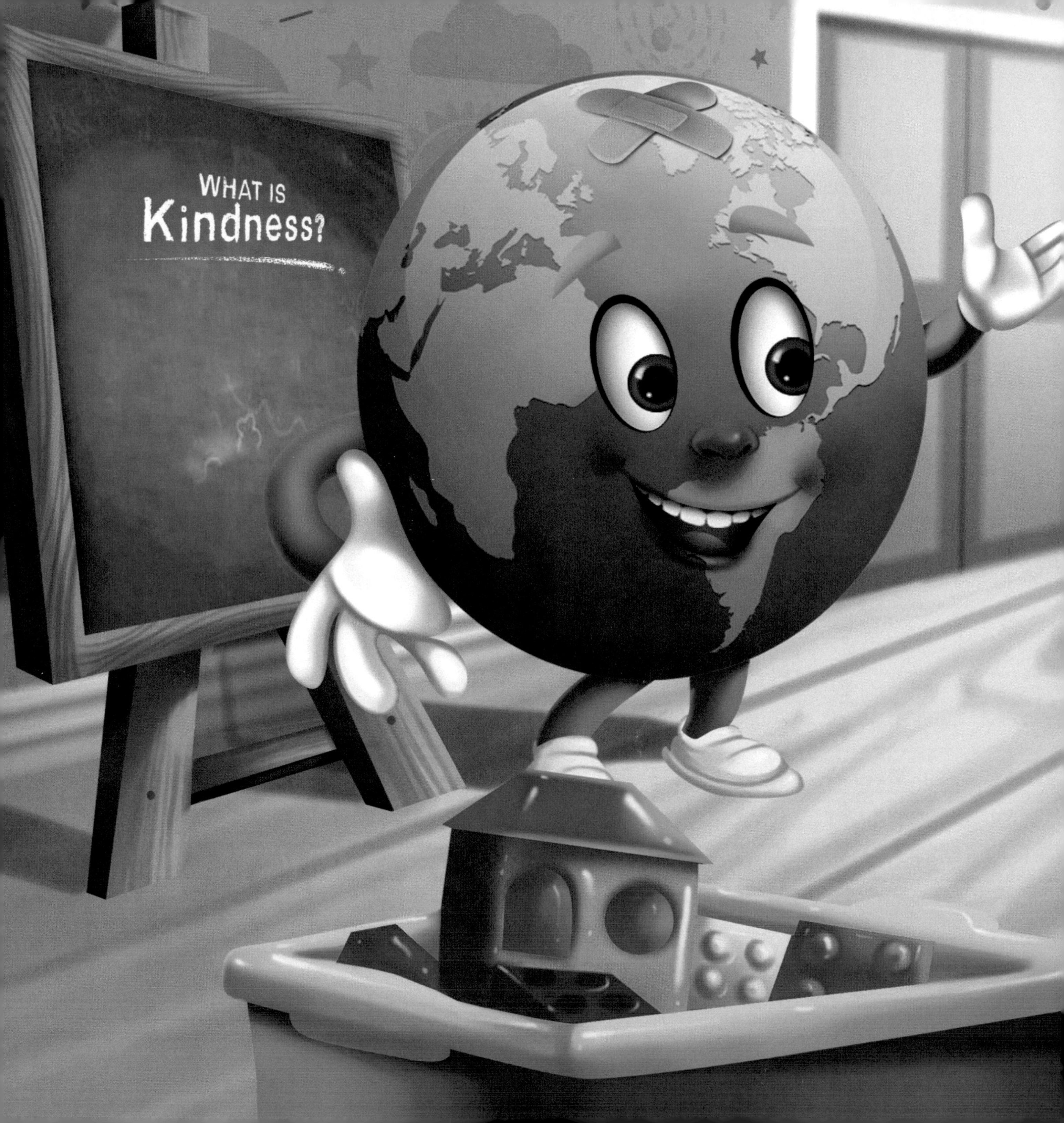
WHAT IS
Kindness?

"Those are excellent answers," says Orbit.
"You are all correct.
Kindness is shown in many ways.
It begins with a choice."

"What's a choice?" asks Jamie. Orbit explains: "Have you ever wanted a toy that someone else was playing with?"

"Yes!" the children shout.

"Okay," says Orbit, "now you have a choice. You can go and grab the toy and take it away,

or you can ask your friend
to please pass it to you
when they are finished
playing with it.
You can CHOOSE
to be kind."

"Sometimes making a **choice** is hard for me," says Dominic.

"Do you know what I do just before I make a choice?" asks Orbit. "I breathe!"

"That's silly," says Sawyer, "everyone breathes."

"Of course we breathe all the time," says Orbit, "but this is my special breathing technique. Let me show you."

Breathe in and slowly raise both arms straight up in the air.

Then hold your breath and keep your arms up as you count to 5.

1 2 3 4 5

Then, as you breathe out, slowly lower your arms until they are level with your shoulders.

This will help you clear your mind and calm your thoughts.

Let's give it try.
1...2...3...4...5...
Ahhh!

"Where have you seen **kindness** in YOUR life?" Orbit asks the class.

Being kind is when Grandma **takes care of us** while our parents **go out for a special night.**

Being kind is welcoming a rescue dog into your family.

Being **kind** is sharing the last chocolate chip cookie, even when you would rather eat the **WHOLE** cookie yourself.

Being **kind** is knowing you have enough, and **donating** to others so they have enough.

Being **kind** is seeing someone behind you and holding the door for them.

Being **kind** is when Mommy makes you chicken soup when you feel sick. Mommy calls that TLC which means Tender Loving Care.

Being **kind** is when **Daddy** plays with you, even when he knows he needs to cut the lawn before it gets dark.

Being **kind** is when your **baby brother** needs a nap, and you choose to do something quiet so he can rest.

Being **kind** is when you see a little girl sitting by herself and ask her if she wants to join you in a game of **jump rope**.

Being kind is reading a book to your baby sister, even if she doesn't understand the entire story.

Being kind is playing Twinkle Twinkle Little Star, the favorite song of a new little girl in daycare who is missing her mommy and daddy.

Being **kind** is saving a **wiggly worm** from drowning.

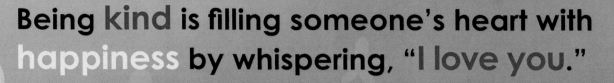

Being **kind** is filling someone's heart with **happiness** by whispering, "I love you."

Can **YOU** think of ways **YOU** can be **kind** to others?

What kindness means is...

These ideas of spreading kindness came from children of families who supported The Power of Kindness Kickstarter.

What kindness means is "I love you and to be a friend."
– Forest Levi Bradley, age 5 Arizona

Where have you seen kindness?
"My friends Hunter and Ella were kind to me. They got popsicles to share with me." – Sawyer DaCosta - age 3.5 Massachusetts

"While sleeping over at my grandma's house, after dinner I helped her with the dishes. It was fun because we got to spend time together and do something we both like to do, organize dishes."
– Amelia Parker - age 6 Rhode Island

Being generous and nice to people, like opening a door for someone. Just simple, little things that make people happy.
– Payton - age 11 Arizona

Helping my teammates at practice. – Tyson - age 9 Arizona

It means being honest and nice. When someone gets hurt, you can ask if they need help, if they're left out you can invite them to play.
– Demi - age 8 Arizona

It means being helpful. – Kameron - age 7 Arizona

It means to listen to your teacher and play with everyone.
– Cali - age 4 Arizona

Hugs! – Brody - age 3 Arizona

"Kindness is sharing beautiful things. We paint and give kindness rocks, which make people happy."
– Hannah - age 5 California

How can you be kind?

I'm kind when I help my mommy with chores. – Malakyh - age 6 Rhode Island

I can be kind to people. – Annabella - age 3 Rhode Island

"Helping someone when they need it."
– Elena - age 9 and Harper - age 6 Connecticut

Thank you for spreading kindness.

About the author

Ruth Maille is a relationship coach and has also owned and operated a daycare/preschool for 30+ years. By using the tools she acquired in both professions, she has had the privilege of helping many families.

Ruth is the author of the multiple award-winning book, **The Power of Positivity**, The ABC's of a Pandemic. Her passion for writing comes from years of reading children's books in both her personal and professional lives. She is grateful for the opportunity to help children learn to use their imaginations to embark on make-believe adventures, and hopes that her books will teach children lifelong values and inspire them to be anything they choose. Ruth is the mom of 3 amazing adults.

This beautifully illustrated story delivers a powerful message about kindness.

About the illustrator

Pardeep Mehra is the founder of Pencil Master Digital Studio, a family-owned business employing a large group of talented artists providing end-to-end illustration and publishing services.

For more than fifteen years, Pardeep has been providing his keen eye and his visualization and digital art skills to create hundreds of beautifully illustrated books that delight children all over the world. Pardeep lives in India with his wife Priyam and daughter Mehar.

For more info and portfolio review, visit
www.pencilmasterdigi.com

73051693R00024